MW00901792

December 2021

To Ella and Mira,

A special story for special sisters!

Brrrrr now cuddle up and

Stay warm and cozy :)

Love
Natty

Karkulka Puppet Theatre
presents:

# The Ice Queen

Dana and Tom Velan

WITH BEST WISHES
FROM Dana & Tom

FriesenPress

Suite 300 - 990 Fort St
Victoria, BC, V8V 3K2
Canada

www.friesenpress.com


First Edition — 2021

This book was inspired by the Snow Queen by Hans Christian Andersen.



ISBN
978-1-5255-9533-2 (Hardcover)
978-1-5255-9532-5 (Paperback)
978-1-5255-9534-9 (eBook)

*1. JUVENILE FICTION, TOYS, DOLLS, PUPPETS*

Distributed to the trade by The Ingram Book Company

For our children Daniel, David, and Michelle,
who inspired the Karkulka Puppet Theatre,
and for our grandchildren, Elle and Liam.

With thanks to our good friend Ingrid for
all the puppet shows we performed together.

# Introduction

A kind old wizard appears in front of the puppet stage dressed in a long blue robe with stars on it and a pointy hat. He is holding a magic cane. Visions of fairy-tale characters surround him.

The wizard raises his hand and says, “Hello, my dear children! Welcome to the Karkulka Puppet Theatre. This little theatre has been entertaining and telling stories to children for nearly forty years. I am the Puppet Wizard and, together with my puppet friends, we are here to tell you a story about two best friends and a mean ice queen.

“This is a story about good and evil, and the power of love and friendship. It was inspired by a fairy tale called *The Snow Queen*, written by the Danish author Hans Christian Andersen about 175 years ago. So, get comfortable, listen to our story, and enjoy the drawings.”

# The Ice Queen

Ella and Jake were best friends and neighbours. It was a few days before Christmas and they were outside decorating a small tree with colourful hand-painted ornaments. Large snowflakes were gently falling the whole day, and everything was white and clean. It was cold, and getting colder!

"It's only three days until Christmas," Ella said, with excitement. "I can't wait! Jake, would you like to come to my house on Christmas Eve for dinner? That's when we celebrate Christmas."

Jake replied, "I would love to! And on Christmas day you can join my family when we celebrate."

"That's great!" said Ella. "It will be like having two Christmases. Jake, you're my best friend."

"And you're my best friend," said Jake. "I hope we will be best friends forever."

"Me, too," Ella said.

As they were placing the **last decorations** on the tree, they noticed a big sled passing by that was being pulled by a reindeer. A serious-looking woman in a long **white dress** was sitting in the sled. Her long hair and dress were **sparkling** in the light like icicles. She was the Ice Queen, the queen of **winter**.

She stopped the sled and looked at the tree that Ella and Jake had just **decorated** with their **favourite** decorations. The Ice Queen did not like Christmas. In a harsh and bitter voice, she spoke:

"I **hate** this Christmas time of year,
I hate the warmth and friendly cheer.
All the hustle, bustle, people, noise,
Giving **charity**, presents, even toys.
The Christmas trees light up the night,
What an **unnatural** and ugly sight.
How I wish and how I pray,
That one such **Christmas day**,
The icy wind will be so freezing,
They won't be **singing**, only sneezing.
The snow and ice will be so thick,
They will forget their Christmas **quick**!"

Jake and Ella looked in **amazement** at the strange lady riding in that sled. Jake called out, "Hello, lady! It's going to be Christmas soon. Halloween was two months ago. When are you going to take off your Halloween costume?" Both children **giggled** at this odd sight.

The Ice Queen got angry and shouted out,

"**Silly children**, haven't you been told?
I am the one who brings the cold!
I bring the ice and snow so deep,
My **icy breath** puts the trees to sleep.
I freeze the lakes and rivers,
I also bring you children **shivers**.
I am the **Ice Queen**! Beware my powers,
I even freeze the hearts of **flowers**."

"I **don't** believe you and I am **not** scared of your silly powers," said Jake bravely. "If you try to freeze my house, I will **light** my wood stove and **melt** your ice into a puddle of water."

Now the Ice Queen was furious with Jake. She pointed her **frosty** fingers at him and shouted, **"How dare you,** little boy! Now **watch** my powers!" and she cast a spell on him with these words:

"You **mock** the Ice Queen for today.
Now you **smile**. Now you **play**.
**No longer** will you be so nice.
Now I turn your heart to **ice**!"

The Ice Queen rode off in her sled, her laugh **echoing** through the falling snow.

After she left, Jake didn't want to play or decorate the tree with Ella **anymore**. He felt cold and strange. He started to shiver.

**"Forget that silly lady,"** said Ella. "She can't really turn your heart to ice. Let's go and play in my house."

"I **don't** want to play in your house," snapped Jake. "And I **don't** want to play with you or anybody else. You **aren't** really my friend, and this is an **ugly** tree."

Ella was upset by Jake's angry outburst and she started to cry. Jake kicked the tree and some decorations fell into the snow. Jake stomped away and Ella ran after him calling, **"Jake! Jake! Wait for me!"**

As Jake walked around town **by himself**, he came upon the Ice Queen's sled. The sled was **empty**, and Jake was cold and tired. He crawled into the sled, covered himself with the thick warm blanket, and **fell asleep**.

Soon the Ice Queen and the reindeer returned. The Ice Queen was happy to find Jake in her sled.

"I could use some **help** around the castle, so **sleep on**, little boy," said the Ice Queen.

**"Reindeer,
come here!
Off to my castle!"**

# In the meantime,

Ella was looking for Jake everywhere. She walked through the empty streets until she came to the edge of town, where the forest started. The forest was very white and quiet, so Ella felt a bit scared being in the forest all alone. Suddenly a rabbit ran by. Then a fox came running past, chasing the rabbit. The rabbit ran quickly through the snow so the fox couldn't catch it.

Ella called out,

## "Jake! Jake! Where are you?"

The fox stopped chasing the **rabbit** and came to ask Ella who she was looking for in the forest on such a **cold** day. "What's the matter, little girl?" asked the fox. "You seem to be **lost**. You don't need to be afraid of me. By the way, have you seen a rabbit running around here? I'm getting mighty **hungry** and that little rabbit keeps hiding and getting away from me."

"You see, Mr. Fox, I am looking for my best friend Jake," said Ella. "There was a mean Ice Queen on an enormous sled who put a **spell** on him. He needs my help!"

The fox said, "I have a friend, a funny-looking reindeer who calls himself **Cariboubou**, and he pulls the sled for the Ice Queen. I saw him pulling the sled today and I remember there was a **boy** sleeping in the back."

"That must be Jake," said Ella. "Do you know where they were going?"

"I don't know for **sure**," said the fox, "**but** I know the place where Cariboubou usually hangs out. I'll try to find him. You stay here, little girl, and keep a look out for that **rabbit**."

"Oh, thank you, Mr. Fox," said Ella. "I hope you can find Cariboubou. I'll watch for the rabbit."

The **reindeer** came to meet Ella. In a goofy-sounding voice, he said, "**Howdy doody,** little girl. Are you the one the fox told me about? Are you looking for a boy who was taken away by the Ice Queenie? I pull the Ice Queenie's sled. I am a reindeer, but my friends call me **Cariboubou.**"

"I am glad Mr. Fox found you," said Ella. "Please, can you take me to see my **best friend** Jake?"

"No problemo. He is at the Ice Castle," said Cariboubou. "I can take you there but **watch out** for the Ice Queenie because she is a big meanie. You can ride on my back."

As they went to the Ice Castle, Cariboubou was happily **rhyming**:

"Lingo bingo, chilli beanie,
Here we come, Ice Queenie.
Christmas cookies, sugar, and **spice**,
This little girl is so very nice.
**Be Nice** Queenie, treat her well,
Help her friend, **release the spell.**"

Cariboubou and Ella arrived at the Ice Castle. In the **courtyard** everything was made of ice. Things looked sparkly and cold. Ella found Jake **cleaning** the Ice Queen's sled.

"**Jake! Jake!** I finally found you," said Ella. "How are you?"

Jake didn't recognize Ella and asked, "Who are you? I don't know you. How come you are so happy? I remember that once I was **happy**, too, but then something happened and I don't remember **anything else**, except that I was very cold. The Ice Queen told me I have to clean this **sled**. I do a lot of work around here, but I feel strange and sad and **lonely**."

Seeing her friend this way made Ella very sad and she started to cry. "Oh, poor, Jake. Don't you **recognize** me? Can't you **remember**?"

Jake said, "Why are you crying?"

Ella hugged Jake and her warm **tears** kept falling on him. Suddenly Jake started to feel strange and **warm**.

Jake looked at his best friend, and his eyes **sparkled**. "Ella! Hi! Where am I? What are you doing here?"

"I came to find you," said Ella. "The mean Ice Queen put a **spell** on you and brought you to her Ice Castle. My hugs and **tears** melted your heart of ice and broke the spell. I am so happy."

"Me too. **Let's go home**," said Jake.

Just at that moment the Ice Queen came out of her castle and started a **blizzard**, so the children couldn't find their way home in the **swirling** snow.

# "What have you done to my little boy?"

**screeched** the Ice Queen.

Jake replied, "Ella has **melted** my heart of ice and now we are going home."

The Ice Queen let out a **terrifying** laugh. "You can't get away from me so easily. Now I will keep **both** of you in my castle. Hey, reindeer, come here and help me **catch** them!"

"Catch them?" asked Cariboubou. "I am getting **sick** and **tired** of you chasing little boys and girls and making them cough and **sneeze**.Ice Queenie, you're an **ice meanie**. Come on, children. Jump up on my back and I will take you **home**!"

They jumped up on Cariboubou and rode off, **leaving** the Ice Queen lost and **all alone** in the swirling white snow.

Ella and Jake were so happy and called out together,

"Yay, Cariboubou! You really showed that mean Ice Queen. Thank you! Now we can go home and have the best Christmas ever! We are so lucky and have so much to be thankful for."

When Ella and Jake came back to their **small town**, they joined the townspeople, children, and animals at the **beautiful** Christmas tree in the middle of the town square. They sang Christmas songs until it got dark. The snow stopped falling and the sky was **clear**, so the stars made a magical backdrop to the lights on the Christmas tree. Ella and Jake were **very happy** and so was their new friend Cariboubou.

# Instructions for cutting out paper puppets:

1. Cut out the next two pages on the dotted line.
2. Cut out the individual front and back of each puppet.
3. Glue the front of the puppet to a thick piece of paper or cardboard.
4. Cut the thick paper or cardboard to the same outline as the puppet.
5. Glue the back of the puppet to the thick paper or cardboard.
6. For extra strength you can glue a popsicle stick to the bottom of the paper puppet.
7. In case of a mistake or if the paper puppet gets lost or damaged, you can download an extra copy from the internet at danavelan.com.

CPSIA information can be obtained
at www.ICGtesting.com
Printed in the USA
BVHW020304300821
615392BV00002B/17

9 781525 595332